LAURA'S STORY

LAURA'S STORY

Written
by Beatrice Schenk
de Regniers

Illustrated by Jack Kent

Atheneum   1979   New York

LIBRARY OF CONGRESS CATALOGING IN PUBLICATION DATA

De Regniers, Beatrice Schenk.
Laura's story.

SUMMARY: Laura tells her mother a bedtime story
about the perilous rescue of a tiny woman.
[1. Mothers and daughters—Fiction]
I. Kent, Jack.   II. Title.
PZ7.D4417Lau   [E]   78-12623
ISBN 0-689-30677-6

"Tell me a story,"
said Laura's mother.

"I'll tell you a true story," Laura said.
"I think it is a true story.
Anyhow, I'll tell it to you.

A long *long* time ago,
I was big and you were little.
Do you remember?"

"I'm not sure," said Laura's mother.
"Tell me about it."

"Well," said Laura, "you were little. You were so little I could put you in my pocket.

You were so little, a soup spoon could be your bathtub."

HERS

"If you wanted
something to eat,
you had to ask me.
I fed you with a
teeny tiny fork."

"What did you give me to eat?" Laura's mother
asked.

"I gave you peanut butter. And one piece of
spaghetti was a big dinner for you.
A little chocolate bit was too much for you
to eat at one time, you were so little.
And when you were bad, I was afraid to spank you.
I was afraid I might squash you like a bug."

"Was I bad very often?" Laura's mother asked.

"No. Just sometimes."
Laura put three chocolate bits in her mouth
all at one time.
"And that's the end of the story."

"The end?" said Laura's mother.
"But nothing happened!"

"Wait till I tell you the next story," Laura said. "Lots of things happen in the next story."

"When will you tell me the next story?" asked Laura's mother.

"Right now," Laura said.

"All right," said Laura's mother. "And after the next story, it will be time to go to bed."

"Well, this is the next story," Laura said.
"And I was still big, and you were still little."

"I remember," Laura's mother said.

"You were so little I put you in my pocket," Laura said.

"You already told me that," Laura's mother said.

"But I had a hole in my pocket," Laura said.
"So I lost you."

"Good heavens!" said Laura's mother.

"Yes," Laura said. "When I got home,
I wanted to take you out of my pocket,
but you weren't there."

"You must have felt terrible," Laura's mother said.

"It was your fault," Laura said.
"You made the hole in my pocket with your
little scissors. And so you fell through the hole.
And so I lost you."

"Did you try to find me?" Laura's mother asked.

"Yes, I tried.
I went back to the park where I was playing.
And I found you sitting on top of a flower."

"Thank goodness!" Laura's mother said.

"But before I could get to you, a big bird
came along and grabbed you."

"Oh help! Did he eat me?" Laura's mother asked.

"No. He flew very high. And he flew over a river, and he let you fall, and . . .

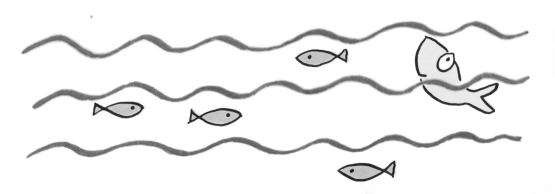

. . . a fish swallowed you whole."

"Thank goodness the fish didn't chew me up,"
Laura's mother said.

"It didn't have any teeth," Laura said.

"And then a big dog jumped into the river and swallowed the fish whole."

"Didn't the dog have any teeth?" asked Laura's mother.

"Stop asking so many questions," Laura said.
"So then an alligator came along . . .

. . . and swallowed the dog whole.

And then . . .

. . . a lion came along and swallowed the alligator whole.
And then an elephant came along and swallowed—"

"I don't believe that," Laura's mother said.
"An elephant could swallow a peanut whole,
or maybe a banana. But not a lion."

"Well, maybe it wasn't an elephant," Laura said.
"But it was a big monster. And it had ears like
an elephant. And . . .

. . . it swallowed the lion whole.''

"Is that the end of the story?"
asked Laura's mother.

"No. And then you sneezed, and that tickled
the fish's stomach, and he coughed you up."

"Thank goodness," said Laura's mother.

"But remember, the fish was inside the dog's stomach," Laura said. "So you sneezed again."

"I must have caught a cold when I fell in the river," said Laura's mother.

"Yes," Laura said. "The water was very cold. Anyhow, you sneezed. And that tickled the dog's stomach, and he coughed you up."

"Thank goodness," Laura's mother said.

"But remember," Laura said,
"the dog was inside the alligator's stomach."

"Oh, yes."

"And you sneezed again."

"I did have a bad cold," Laura's mother said.

"Well," Laura said, "when you sneezed,

". . . that tickled the alligator's stomach,
and he coughed you up,
and you were in the lion's stomach.
And you sneezed again,
and that tickled the lion's stomach,
and he coughed you up,
and you were in the monster's stomach.

"And then you sneezed again, and that tickled
the monster, and he coughed you up."

"And then you picked me up and took me home," said Laura's mother.

"How did you know that?" Laura asked.

"Because that is what I would do if I were big and you were little," said Laura's mother. "And I would give you a hug and a kiss."

"That's what I did," Laura said. "I took you home and gave you some warm soup."

"What kind of soup?" Laura's mother asked.

"Spaghetti soup," Laura said.

"Mmm. My favorite soup," said Laura's mother.

And Laura didn't say anything because . . .

Laura was sound asleep.